D1644439

This LITTLE MAMMOTH belongs to

_____

_____

_____

Frog, Duck and Rabbit

Frog, Duck and Rabbit

Susanna Gretz

LITTLE
MAMMOTH

Frog, Duck, and Rabbit are making a costume.

"It will need wheels," says Duck. "I'll get my skates."

"Stupid skates," says Rabbit.
"They're not," says Duck.

"Your feet look stupid, too," says Rabbit.

"They don't," says Duck.

"Flatfoot, Flatfoot!" says Frog. "And if you're having wheels, so am I."

Frog gets her scooter.
"Stupid scooter," says Duck.
"It isn't," says Frog.

"Your bottom looks stupid, too," says Duck.

"It doesn't," says Frog.

"Spottybum, Spottybum!" says Rabbit.

"And if you're having wheels, so am I."

Rabbit gets his skateboard.
"Stupid skateboard," says Frog.
But Rabbit isn't bothered.

"Your ears look stupid, too," says Frog.
Rabbit still isn't bothered.

"Flopears, Flopears!" says Duck.
Now Rabbit *is* bothered.
"Don't call me that," he says.

"Anyway," says Frog, "*you* started the teasing, Rabbit."
"No I didn't," says Rabbit.
"Yes, you did, Flopears!"

"My name isn't Flopears!" yells Rabbit.
"Flopears, Flopears!" yell Duck and Frog.

FLOPEARS FLOPEARS

FLOPEARS FLOPEARS

"STOP!" wails Rabbit.

Suddenly, they remember the costume.
"It's nearly time for the parade," says Duck.

"And we haven't even started on the costume,"
moans Rabbit.
"Let's get busy," says Frog.

They work very hard.

Finally the costume is ready.

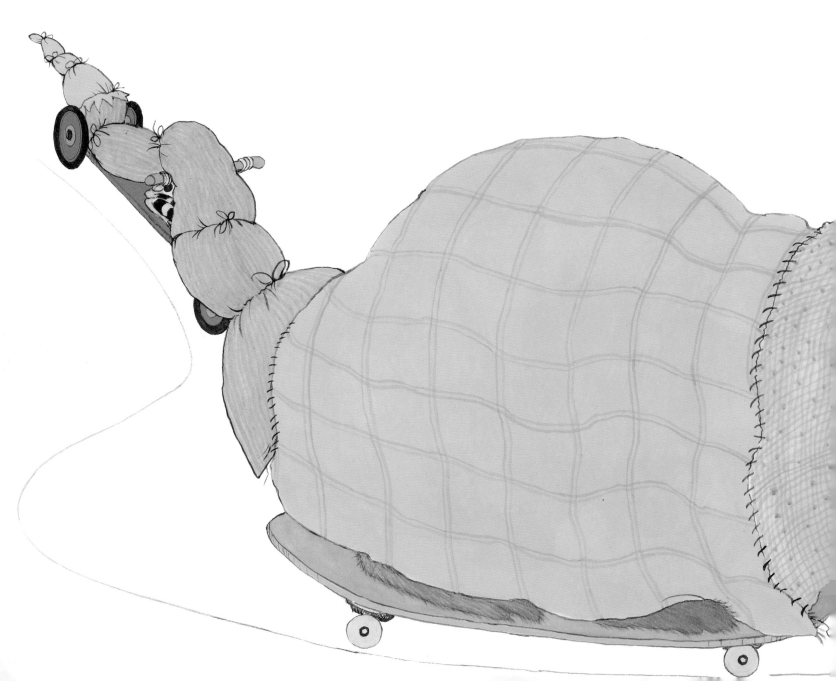

It's the best crocodile...

. . . in the whole parade.

Everyone admires the costume on wheels.
"Did you make it yourselves?" they ask.
"Yes," says Rabbit. "It was made by Flatfoot,
Spottybum..."

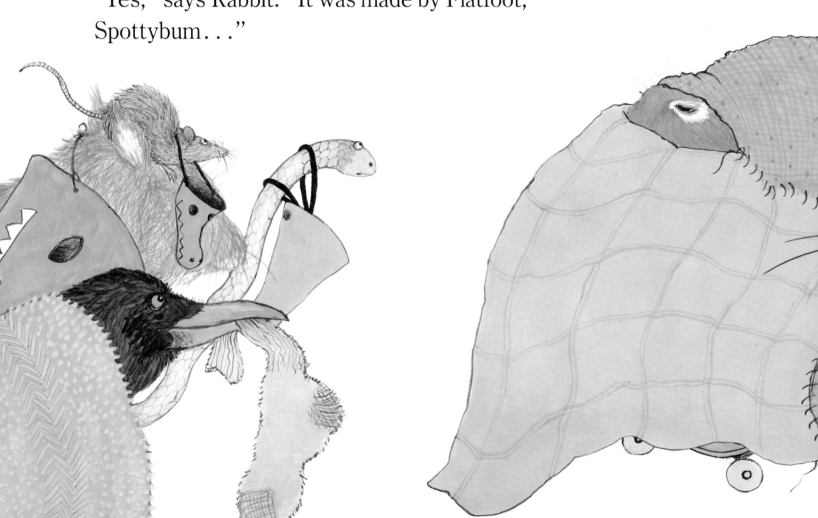

"What?" yell Duck and Frog.

"... and Flopears," says Rabbit.

And then Flatfoot, Spottybum and Flopears went home for their tea.

First published in Great Britain 1992
by Methuen Children's Books Ltd
Published 1993 by Little Mammoth
an imprint of Reed Consumer Books Ltd
Michelin House, 81 Fulham Road, London SW3 6RB
and Auckland, Melbourne, Singapore and Toronto

Copyright © 1992 by Susanna Gretz

The right of Susanna Gretz to be identified as author of this work
has been asserted by her in accordance with the
Copyright, Designs and Patents Act 1988

ISBN 0 7497 1299 6

A CIP catalogue record for this title
is available from the British Library

Printed in Great Britain
by Scotprint Ltd, Musselburgh, Scotland

LITTLE
MAMMOTH